This TWO HOOTS
book belongs to

For Freya

This edition published 2020 by Two Hoots
First published 2019 by Two Hoots
an imprint of Pan Macmillan
The Smithson, 6 Briset Street, London EC1M 5NR
Associated companies throughout the world
www.panmacmillan.com

ISBN 978-1-5098-3456-3

With thanks to Suzanne Carnell, Helen Weir, Jo Spooner and Sharon King-Chai

www.twohootsbooks.com

1 3 5 7 9 8 6 4 2
A CIP catalogue record for this book is available from the British Library.
Printed in China
The illustrations in this book were created using paint, ink, brush pens and china markers.

MAISIE PARADISE SHEARRING

I'M ACTUALLY REALLY GROWN-UP NOW

TWO HOOTS

Meena did NOT want to go to bed.

"That's because we're grown-ups, Meena," Dad sighed. "You know we go to bed a bit later."

But when Dad had gone, Meena crept out of bed to watch the party. Everyone was having so much fun without her. It wasn't fair.

Meena began to hatch a plan.

The next morning, Meena made a very important announcement to her family.

"Tonight I'm going to have my very own grown-up party, and you can both come."

"I'm going to be so good at grown-up things.
Look, I made you a special breakfast!"

Being a grown-up was going to be fun!

First, Meena decided to
borrow some grown-up
clothes from Mum.

She tried everything she knew grown-ups liked wearing.

When she was sure everything was just right, she shouted . . .

I'm ready!

At breakfast Meena and Mum caught up on the latest news.

Then Meena brushed her teeth, packed her pencil crayons, and jumped into the car to go to work like Mum.

The traffic was a nightmare, so Meena decided it would be best to work at home with Dad.

Dad needed a lot of help with his garden designs.
Meena came up with some great new ideas.
She was very good at drawing slugs and snails.

Once Meena's plans were ready, she headed outside to make her new garden.

Being a grown-up was easy, she thought.

Soon it was time for Meena to start planning her party. There was lots to do. First she had to find some guests.

Meena invited Bob, Leah and Seb, from next door. Bob and Leah were playing birds.

It did look a tiny bit fun, but Meena hoped they wouldn't play like this at her grown-up party.

Next, Meena took her Dad to the shop to get party things.

Come on now, Meena. We've not got much time. Mum'll be home from work soon.

When they got home, Dad said that a very grown-up thing to do was to help unpack the shopping from the car . . .

. . . and to put the food away,

and to tidy her toys, ready for the party.

Some parts of being a grown-up weren't that easy after all, and definitely not fun.

At last, the guests arrived and it was party time!

Fruit anyone?
Can't we play a game?
I hate fruit

I don't like grown-up parties

Meena wasn't sure if grown-ups cried,
but she thought she might.

Meena went outside to tell everyone the party was over.

What were they all doing? It didn't look very grown-up . . .

. . . but it did look like a lot of fun.

Meena decided to stop being a grown-up for the time being. And guess what?

So did her mum and dad!

CHOC

A note from the author

Maisie Paradise Shearring is an illustrator and author who lives in Hull, in the North of England. Just like Meena, Maisie has her very own cat (Maisie's cat is called Bunk). Lots of the stories and pictures Maisie makes are drawn from her own experiences. In fact, when Maisie was a child, she once asked her mum to stop the car because she had a very important announcement to make – "I'm actually really grown-up now!" Meena's joy and enthusiasm are inspired by Maisie's nephew, Noah, who was four when this book was made.

Can you count all the bananas in this book? There are lots! Bananas have been Maisie's favourite snack since she was a child, but she has never used one to make a phone call.